Undying Embers of God's Love

Lead Me Safely Through the Perils in Life
Book 1

JANET F. ROBINSON

UNDYING EMBERS OF GOD'S LOVE
A book of poetry, scripture, and spiritual thoughts
Copyright © 2023 by Janet F. Robinson

Cover design: Sharon Kizziah-Holmes

All Scripture quotations used in this book are from the King James Version of the Bible.
Printed in the United States of America

Valera Press

ISBN -13: 979-8-9861694-0-8

Dedication

To my father, Louis Martin, whom I deeply love and admire; he has been a good example to me. When I was a child, he planted the seed of God's love in me. Listening to him has helped me more fully understand the depth of God's love. When I was going through the emotional trauma of a divorce, he was helping me instead of criticizing me. His love has never failed.

~ ~ ~

To my Father in Heaven for His undying love for me; He has made it possible for the light in my life to shine into the hearts of others. His love has never failed.

TABLE OF CONTENTS

Preface

TO ENRICH OUR RELATIONSHIP

We can miss the mark completely as to the theme of the Scriptures and of Christ in our life. Our relationship with Christ becomes very shallow and stagnant because we do not know how to open up and give our heart and our life to Christ. We may have gone to church all our life, yet we don't have a deep commitment to Christ. We only believe what we are taught, and then we are not sure if we are right or wrong. We feel there is something missing in our relationship with Christ. We have no desire to change, to be different, to become like Christ.

The purpose for which I have written these thoughts is that we might know how to give our heart and our life to Christ—to follow Him and only Him—that we might have a desire to become Christlike, and that we might experience a deeper and a more meaningful relationship with Christ. We then can begin to see the whole theme throughout the Scriptures and the full essence of Christianity, which is love—God's undying love for you and for me.

For God so loved the world, that he gave his only begotten
Son, that whosoever believeth
in him should not perish, but have everlasting life.
John 3:16

We believe in Christ, we love Him, and we believe He can save us from our sins.

Introduction

The ability to express myself through writing this book is a gift from God because I have never been able to open up and express my inner thoughts and feelings before in my entire life. The manner and purpose for which I use this self-expression is my gift back to God.

THIS PART OF MY HEART I GIVE TO YOU

It is my hope, as you read these letters of love written from my heart, that a spark might be kindled in you, which will turn into a glow and light up your entire life—you might come to know Christ—so that you can rise above the trials and difficulties you face with God's saving power—the power of God's love.

Wherefore I desire that ye faint not at my tribulations for you, which is your glory.
For this cause I bow my knees unto the Father of our Lord Jesus Christ, Of whom
the whole family in heaven and earth is named, That he would grant you, according
to the riches of his glory, to be strengthened with might by his Spirit in the inner man;
That Christ may dwell in your hearts by faith; that ye, being rooted and grounded in love,
May be able to comprehend with all saints what is the breadth, and length,
and depth, and height; And to know the love of Christ, which passeth knowledge,
that ye might be filled with all the fulness of God. Now unto him that is able to
do exceeding abundantly above all that we ask or think, according to the

power that worketh in us, Unto him be glory in the church
by Christ Jesus
throughout all ages, world without end. Amen.
Ephesians 3:13–21

Turning Point

Ask, and it shall be given you; seek, and ye shall find;
knock, and it shall be opened unto you.

Matthew 7:7

My son, despise not the chastening of the LORD; neither be
weary of his correction: For whom the LORD loveth he
correcteth; even as a father the son in whom he delighteth.

Proverbs 3:11–12

THE CHALLENGE

Sometimes we are taken to the depths of despair in life so
that we will want to reach out to God and follow only Him.

These are the times in our life that Christ challenges us.
He is saying to you, and He is saying to me, "I dare you to
pick yourself up out of the miry clay of sin—those sins of
bitterness, resentment, and guilt. I dare you to get right with
God. I dare you to have total commitment. I dare you to
strive to become your best and be all you can be in the
Lord."

THY WILL—NOT MY WILL

Lord, I have tried to make all the decisions in my life. I have had to have my own way. But I have reached a point of deep despair where I want You to be in complete control of my life. I want Your way with me.

Submit yourselves therefore to God.

James 4:7

Submit: give our heart to God and trust in Him to lead us.

DEEP COMMITMENT

Well, Lord, here I am. I am finally ready to listen to You. I finally want You to make all the decisions for me in my life. I am finally ready to follow You wherever You lead me. I am ready. Let us begin.

WHERE DO I BEGIN?

When our workload is stacked high at our job—we cannot see the top of our desk—we become loaded down. We do not stop; we keep going, starting at the bottom and working our way to the top until we can see our desk—the work is done—and we are all caught up.

When our problems stack up in life and weigh us down, we feel lost. We do not know where to begin. We grab hold of ourselves and reach out to God. We start at the bottom, working out each problem one at a time. Christ helps us carefully sort each problem. He helps us understand where we are wrong. We strive to overcome. We take on a new attitude. It is not too late. We can begin now—we can overcome—and we will change for Him.

GIFT OF WISDOM

If we could have anything we asked for, would it be wisdom? That was what Solomon asked for. We may reach a point in life where we need to know what is right and what is wrong.

Yea, if thou criest after knowledge, and liftest up thy voice for understanding;
If thou seekest her as silver, and searchest for her as for hid treasures; Then
shalt thou understand the fear of the LORD, and find the knowledge of God.
For the LORD giveth wisdom: out of his mouth cometh knowledge and
understanding. He layeth up sound wisdom for the righteous.

Proverbs 2:3–7

My religious beliefs have always been a strict obedience to the letter of God's law. When divorce shattered all my beliefs, I asked myself, "Am I still a Christian? I have broken the letter of God's law." I then found myself reaching out to God and asking Him for His wisdom in the direction I should take in my life. I did not want to be lost eternally, and I did not want to become a bitter person. I received this answer from Him, "You are the one who needs to change."

That is it. That was where I had been wrong. That was what had been missing in my life. I needed to change to become more like Christ. I had tried my best to obey His principles, but I needed to open myself up to Him, become like Him, and live like Him.

ACCEPTING CHANGE

We resent it if someone comes barging into our life screaming, "You have to change!"

We scream back, "No, I don't!"

"But, if you are a Christian, you must change. You cannot be you—you must be someone you are not."

"No, I don't want to change. I like me the way I am. How can I be someone I am not? I am me, and you are you. Accept me, and I will accept you, then we can live together in peace."

"But you have to change."

"No, I will not. The only way I would ever change is if I wanted to change. It is not anything anyone could force me to do. If I wanted to change, I could, and I would do it on my own."

Voices have lowered.

"Are you a Christian?"

"Yes."

"Do you want to become more like Christ?"

"Yes."

Voices have changed to a more kind and gentle tone.

"We, as Christians, are always changing. We are striving daily to become more like Christ in our life. We work at having peace, joy, kindness, gentleness, patience, self-control, faithfulness, goodness, and love in our life. We are trying to be our best—to change to become more like Him. It means not only change for you but for me as well."

"Oh, well in that case, I'm all for it."

TO BECOME CHRISTLIKE

Transforming ourselves requires willingness and a desire to change. It takes time and energy. Sometimes it requires changing our behavioral patterns that have been established since childhood. It is reaching out beyond what we set as our own expected limitations as a person. It is setting Christ as our goal—to become like Him.

We begin to realize we have a learning capacity that never ceases. It is growing as an individual, in our personality, and spiritually. Christ is our motivating factor. He is our inner source of strength. We are to become different—beautiful in our hearts for Him.

And be not conformed to this world: but be ye transformed by the
renewing of your mind.

Romans 12:2

Conform: be the person that others think we should be so we will be accepted.

Transform: change into a better version of ourselves.

CONFORM OR TRANSFORM?

When we *conform*, we are trying to fit ourselves into a personality that someone else has created for us (what they think a Christian ought to be): how we should feel, how we should act, how we should look, and how we should think. We are trying our best to be the person the world thinks a Christian should be. When we conform to their standard, Jesus becomes just a person we read about—He existed in another era of time. And our lives are still the same: we feel empty. We have taken a wrong turn in our spiritual life. We are letting others rule in our life instead of Jesus. We are trying our best—we are sincere—and we do not know any different.

When we *transform*, change comes from within. It is a desire to change to become like Christ. It is casting off the old and putting on the new. We are different from the world because our personality is loving, caring, and sharing. Jesus is no longer a person we just read about—He comes alive in our life, He bridges the gap, and He is our link to *LIFE*. Our life becomes centered around Him. The empty vessel we live in is filled. Jesus is our great example. He is our pattern for living. He is saying to you and me, "Come as you are, and grow with Me toward perfection."

To Think Strong Is to Be Strong

I can do all things through Christ which strengtheneth me.

Philippians 4:13

Strength is the distinct quality that separates one person from another.

~ ~ ~

After my divorce, I struggled with many feelings of grief, fear, and loneliness. I started searching for answers to my questions. When I reached out to God, He gave me answers to those questions. He helped heal me from my emotional wounds, and He put the song back into my life so I could move on.

~ ~ ~

Life is full of ups and downs, but when we live our life

in Christ, we know we are on our way up.

GRIEF UNSPOKEN

Grief:
It doesn't knock. It enters at the most
    inopportune and least expected
    moment.
Wherever it goes, it leaves a trail of sadness,
    loneliness, and bitterness to hearts
    that are broken.
It knows no joy.
It knows only pain that cuts like a knife
    clear through—pain, ceaseless,
    unending.

Oh, hearts that are stricken down with
    sorrow—weep.
You need to grieve, but don't grieve alone,
find another heart to share your sadness,
and together you both can become strong.

I had been married to my ex-husband for only eight
months when he received military orders to serve in the
Vietnam War.

WAR

You are an enemy of love.
You take our youth and fill their hearts with
    hate.
You teach our youth to kill. How can you
    kill without hate in your heart?
You fill our youth with emotional problems

they cannot handle because they
have never known your way before.

You are hated by:
Every mother who has lost a son to you.
Every wife who has lost a husband to you.
Every soldier who comes home without an
    arm or a leg.

You bring many husbands home closed and
    distant because this is their only way
    of blocking you out.
You are the reason why many marriages
    fail—creating more bitterness and
    hate.
Your way is fast.
Your way is destructive.

You have a way of changing people's lives.
    Their lives are never the same again.
Yes, you are to blame
for many hate-filled hearts.
You are a big price to pay.

~ ~ ~

I love my country. The freedom I have to express my
belief in Christ and teach others is essential in my life. I
would fight for this freedom. I would die for it.
Let us pray for continued peace with other nations.

FEAR

You are in complete control of my life.
I don't know how to overcome you.
I take only a few risks in life because I am
    afraid.
I am tormented by you day and night.

Aah! I have found a way to get rid of you.
You no longer entangle me in your web—
for my personal relationship with my Lord
    and my Savior
has grown to a point beyond all fear.

LONELINESS

You sweep over me and engulf me.
I may be alone or in a crowd.
You are a bitter cup to partake of.
I know of no one who has not come in full
    view of you.

You blind my vision, and temptations sneak
    up on me.
I would like to do those things I know I
    should not.
Oh, Lord, please keep Your presence strong
    in my life
so that I may overcome this lonely, aching
    heart.

~ ~ ~

Our heart may be good, but sometimes it is tried, tested, and broken before it can become its best.

PUTTING THE SONG BACK INTO OUR LIVES

When the song has gone out of our life, we feel we are a person with no name—a person with nothing to live for. We feel hurt, rejected, and our spirit is broken.

We pick ourselves up, keep going, and look to God with faith in our heart to put the song back into our life.

With faith comes hope, and we begin listening to those around us—those who really care about us. They help us believe in ourselves. This is a time in our life when we believe God sends these people to lift us up—to keep us going.

When the song starts coming back into our life, we become stronger than ever. We begin to sing a new song. We want to sing it to others. We want to help others put the song back into their lives—we want to reach out and show them we believe in them—we believe they have potential—they can make it in life.

~ ~ ~

When we try to work everything out in our lives by ourselves and we just can't seem to get it all together, I believe God is trying to tell us to get back in touch with Him and let Him work it out for us.

~ ~ ~

In our storms of life, Jesus is the rock that we lean on.

He is our strength. We cling to Him. By putting all our faith and trust in Him, He becomes our only hope. We realize that only through Him can we ever hope to have eternal salvation.

YE SHALL KNOW THEM BY THEIR FRUITS

Jesus is the vine, and we are the branches. When we become more mature in Christ, we can bear precious fruit for our Lord and Savior—fruits of love, joy, and peace. Sometimes in our life we, as Christians, become barren. We cannot grow spiritually because we are walled in by our own traditional backgrounds. We cannot see beyond what we have been taught. We do not have understanding in our heart for others.

God loves us, and He sees that for us to grow spiritually He will have to prune us—cut us back. He allows us to go through pain and suffering in our life. This makes us into a stronger branch. Through the pain and suffering in our life, we can grow spiritually.

Only when we have an understanding heart can we experience love, joy, and peace in our life.

A TIME FOR HEALING

We open up our inner feelings and our deep needs to those we love and trust.

When we have been hurt or when we need to be healed emotionally, we can go to God anytime. When we open up to God, we trust in Him to help us find where the problems lie in our life. When we become mature enough to forgive ourselves and others, God leads the way for healing in our life.

~ ~ ~

Man finds it hard to forgive and to forget. One of the hardest things for us to realize is that God does forgive, and He does forget if we ask.

~ ~ ~

Your adversary the devil, as a roaring lion, walketh about, seeking whom he may devour.

1 Peter 5:8

THE SPIRITUAL SLUMP

We all experience this. It is Satan's way of attacking our faith. We begin listening to the negative thoughts and attitudes around us, and soon we are caught up in the negative. This should be a warning signal. We should stop and think.

The light within us is becoming dimmer, and Satan would love to blow it out. It is up to us to turn our attitudes around, think positively, and keep the inner light within us strong and in full glow.

DETERMINATION IS . . .

Thinking we can do it—
working at it
until we have done it.

THINKING POSITIVELY

I was told I couldn't do it.

I replied, "Yes, I can."

WALKING TALL

Lord,
Help me walk with my head held high.
Help me not to be afraid of the dark.
Let me keep my hand in Your hand.
Let me stand beside You and walk tall
    through life.

Look Beyond This Day

Look up. Look around. Let us look beyond ourselves and give to others.

And we know that all things work together for good to them
that love God,
to them who are the called according to his purpose.

Romans 8:28

Life goes on after divorce. I asked myself, "What happens to me now?" I found myself thinking about spiritual freedom, and there was that pivotal moment when I realized I could still dream.

~ ~ ~

Yesterday is gone—today is here. This day can be the beginning of a new tomorrow in our life.

~ ~ ~

PUTTING THE PAST BEHIND

I believe if my Lord and Savior should choose us on Judgment Day, He will choose us for what we have become and not for what we have been in our past.

~ ~ ~

He hath set me free . . .

And ye shall know the truth, and the truth shall make you free.

John 8:32

REAL FREEDOM

When I was a teenager, I read this Scripture, and I could not understand it. When I was in my twenties, I read this Scripture, and I still could not understand it. In my thirties, and after going through a divorce and a difficult time, I began to have an understanding of this Scripture. I can understand these things now because of where I have been in life.

I was at the bottom in life, and I reached out to God: "Please save me from this miserable state of mind that I am in. I want more out of my life. I will put my faith and my trust in You, dear Lord. I know You love me because You died for me. I will change for You because I love You. I have a desire to become better. I want to be a happy person."

This is when I began to feel my heart changing. I became spiritually alive. When I read the Scriptures, I started to understand them for the first time in my life. I felt the Spirit working in my life and teaching me spiritual truths.

The Spirit of truth, is come, he will guide you into all truth.
John 16:13

I began to realize that this is at the heart of all truth: Jesus is the Christ. As I reached for Him, I felt His love for me. His atoning sacrifice became real to me, and I began to feel the power from the redeeming blood of His atoning sacrifice within me. It is the power to change from within. This change within me has given me freedom—freedom to grow spiritually, freedom to think for myself, and freedom to become a better person.

My thinking pattern has changed. These are some of the changes from how I used to think to how I now think:

- We are free in Christ—free to be ourselves and free to love God and worship God from our heart. We are no longer bound by the shackles of sin that once held us back. We realize we had become slaves to fear, pride, jealousy, envy, and strife.
- We are free to worship God no matter where we are, every minute, every hour of every day of our

life.

- We are free to be loving and kind, even to the very lowliest of people, hoping in our heart that they will see something in us that will make them want to change their lifestyle.

- We are free to be our own person. We know God accepts us as we are (we may be at the very bottom in life), then from there, with a strong desire in our heart to please God, we strive to reach our highest potential in life by always glorifying Him.

- We are free to think for ourselves. We can study and go directly to God for guidance in our life. We can search the Scriptures ourselves. We do not have to be told what we can and cannot do— we are following Christ. He is our guide. We are allowed to grow spiritually. Nothing blocks us from the closeness we feel to God. In the insecurity of our old way of life, it was easier for someone else to tell us how and where to worship and how we, as Christians, were supposed to feel, look, and act. It was possible that we could become slaves to groups and organizations. It was much easier to let someone else think for us and tell us what to do. That way, the responsibility was on someone else's shoulders. It was possible for preachers to become gods to us. We tried to please them instead of our Father in Heaven. With this new life in Christ, we have a responsibility to think for ourselves and teach others. In our new way of life our behavior is a result of our relationship with Christ.

In our old way of thinking, our relationship with Christ was purely physical—we had to be at every church service, we had to give more money for bigger church buildings, we had to knock on doors to bring in bigger crowds, we could not fellowship with certain groups. If we did not conform, we were made to feel guilty.

In our new way of life, we realize our relationship with Christ is purely inner. It starts within our heart and works outward to others. We are free to grow spiritually. We look forward to meeting with our brothers and sisters in Christ. If there is a need, we are glad to give.

God loves us very much (this very minute). He gave His only begotten Son long ago so we might be set free from sin. He made it possible for us to grow into a true love for God; this love is like a total eclipse: it blocks out all our sin, fear, guilt, and strife. Our slate can be wiped clean, and a new life can begin for each of us. All we have to do is extend to God our love, our willingness, and our desire to be the person He wants us to be. Only then will we ever be able to change our heart for Him.

When our heart begins to change, we feel love and kindness toward others. We begin to have an understanding for others. With the love we feel in our heart for God and for others, we know we have been set free.

A new heart also will I give you, and a new spirit will I put

within you:
and I will take away the stony heart out of your flesh.

Ezekiel 36:26

TO BE SET FREE

You cannot catch love and put it in a box.
Some have tried and have seen it wither and
   die right before their eyes.
Love cannot be caught.
Love must have the freedom to grow.

Love that is of God offers the
freedom to be oneself,
freedom to be expressed,
freedom to flow from one heart to another,
freedom to become,
and freedom to rise in search of new
   horizons.

This kind of love is free to love.
It is loving others even if others do not love
   us.

Where the Spirit of the Lord is, there is liberty.

2 Corinthians 3:17

A NEW BIRTH—A NEW CREATION

God, help me burst out of this box, this empty shell, this void tomb that surrounds me where only fear lurks and emptiness dwells. Help me escape through the barriers—those barriers that have been created in my mind by myself and by others. Help me burst forth and become a new creation so I can fly with the power of Your liberating freedom, the freedom that man has fought and died for, the freedom of Your love.

~ ~ ~

Opening up to God's love is first discovering the real us deep inside ourselves—realizing we are each special, unique—then liking the special person we are. We can then open ourselves up to God and to others.

LIFT THE VEIL

A closed mind creates a closed heart.
A closed heart is like
drawing a curtain over our heart.
It becomes a veil to our understanding.

THE ACHIEVERS

HEY! I still have my life to live. Just because yesterday is nonexistent does not mean I have to be.
I want to live.
I can still dream.

> I want to reach for the stars. I want to help those who hurt look beyond their hurt.
>
> I want to help others reach for the stars too.

LIMITED GROWTH?

We quit growing as an individual when we reach a point of maturity that lives up to the expectation of our family and friends. When God becomes our Heavenly Father, we can grow as an individual and we can grow spiritually beyond all our own, or our family's, expectations.

DARE TO DREAM

> I believe our dreams
> become God's dreams for us
> when we let Him into our heart—
> when we let Him reign in our life.

Faith with Works of Love

Faith which worketh by love.

Galatians 5:6

Faith without works is dead.

James 2:20

As I travel my faith-filled journey through life, the Spirit teaches me many spiritual lessons along the way.

YES, I CAN MAKE IT!

Once we are set free from the sin that bound us, our life becomes a pilgrimage of faith from now to eternity. Step-by-step, each mountain we cross, each valley we enter, each hill we climb, every detour in our path, we know we can make it through because Christ is leading us on— higher and higher we go. Around every bend in the road, we think positively. We know that, if we can make it, there lies glory ahead. We have a hope that just keeps hoping, a trust that just keeps trusting; we have a love that just won't die.

The higher we go, the stronger our faith becomes. Our faith comes alive. It is a working faith. It is active, reaching out; we want to share this faith with others. Negative thoughts can no longer penetrate our mind. They are not even allowed (for this faith has become a rock). We know that if we endure to the end, we shall receive a crown of righteousness, glory, and honor, and we shall live with our Lord and Savior forever.

~ ~ ~

Faith conquers fear.

God is love; and he that dwelleth in love dwelleth in God, and God in Him.

1 John 4:16

DOES GOD REALLY EXIST?

Oh, Lord, help me teach my children (even though they do have faith and believe) when they have those creeping moments of doubt and fear and they ask, "How do we know there is a God?"

Lord, please help me reply in words they can understand: "If you feel any love inside of you at all, the part of you that loves is God. And, if you have any love in your heart, the love you feel is proof enough of God's existence, for God is love."

DEPENDENCY OR TRUST?

When we depend on the Lord to save us, we feel that the Lord will save us because of who we are. We tend to think that God owes us a home in heaven for the good we have done. It is an expectancy based on what we do.

When we trust in the Lord to save us, we feel that regardless of who we are or where we have been in life, we can be saved. We put our confidence in, we hope for, and we believe in Jesus and His power to save—we trust in Him, that He will save us.

THE GREAT TEACHER STILL EXISTS

Life is one big classroom, and Christ, the Great Teacher, is our schoolmaster when we let Him lead us.

We can learn from other people. We can learn from our mistakes. We can parallel our everyday life with those characters in the Bible of long ago and learn from them as to how they handled situations. We can learn to find good in everything.

PSALM TWENTY-THREE

The LORD is my shepherd. He is my guide, He is my life, He watches over me.

I shall not want. In Him, there is no need.

He maketh me to lie down in green pastures. I marvel at the beauty that surrounds me.

He leadeth me beside the still waters. I feel peace within.

He restoreth my soul: he leadeth me in the paths of righteousness for his name's sake. He lifts me up and sets me back on the right path. He leads me in a path that goes upward.

Yea, though I walk through the valley of the shadow of death, I will fear no evil: for thou art with me; thy rod and thy staff they comfort me. Even in the storms of my life I have no fear—the Lord has not left me.

Thou preparest a table before me in the presence of mine enemies: thou anointest my head with oil; my cup runneth over. The world no longer threatens me, for His love has made me strong.

Surely goodness and mercy shall follow me all the days of my life: and I will dwell in the house of the LORD for ever. We are promised a bright and shining future. He will take us home with Him, and we will stay there forever.

And whoso trusteth in the LORD, happy is he.
Proverbs 16:20

Believing in Jesus and trusting in Him to lead me brings happiness to my heart.

TRUE HAPPINESS

True happiness can be found in releasing all our fears, troubles, cares, hopes, and dreams of this world to Him and trusting Him enough to lead us, even if the road may appear steep and rocky and others will not follow for fear. We may stumble and fall at times, and sometimes the path seems to be misleading.

We must turn our whole life over to the Lord and let Him lead us. Each day is exciting. We do not know what is going to happen next in our life. This truly is an adventure in the Lord.

We have faith enough to follow Him without any fear because we know He knows what is best for us, and if we stand firm and follow in His path—this path leads upward—He shall give us a home in heaven forever.

~ ~ ~

When we receive something that is free to us, we do not place as great a value on it as we would if we had to work hard, save our money, and pay a large price in order to obtain it.

A SOUL BOUGHT FOR A PRICE

Our souls were bought for a price—
Christ gave His life for us.
He suffered, bled, and died for you and for
    me.
Our souls are that valuable to Him.

Is it asking too much of us to . . .
Work hard to remain steadfast in the faith
    even though we have pain, sorrow,
    loneliness, financial crises, and
    unfortunate circumstances in our
    life?
Save ourselves for Him, and try our best to
    remain pure from sin?
Pay whatever price in life we must pay in
    order to steer ourselves from the
    pitfalls of Satan?

Reach Out

Put on the whole armour of God, that ye may be able to stand against the
wiles of the devil. For we wrestle not against flesh and blood, but against
principalities, against powers, against the rulers of the darkness of this world,
against spiritual wickedness in high places. Wherefore take unto you the
whole armour of God, that ye may be able to withstand in the evil day,
and having done all, to stand. Stand therefore, having your loins girt
about with truth, and having on the breastplate of righteousness;
And your feet shod with the preparation of the gospel of peace; Above all,
taking the shield of faith, wherewith ye shall be able to quench all the
fiery darts of the wicked. And take the helmet of salvation, and the sword

of the Spirit, which is the word of God.

Ephesians 6:11–17

I have come to the realization that we are in a war between good and evil in this life.

LAUNCHING OUT INTO THE DEEP

We are to clothe ourselves with the armor of God. We go forward in faith not knowing what lies ahead in our life. We are not to look back—we are not to live in our past—we are to look to our future. Christ is our almighty shepherd. We trust in Him to lead us. Our life becomes a challenge of love conquering hate. Anything or anyone that threatens our close relationship with God becomes our enemy, for our commitment to God is a deep conviction in our heart.

~ ~ ~

It is our choice to be free in Christ, but to be free, we must be strong. We must be ready to meet the challenges that are sure to come our way. If we are weak, we will be instantly dominated by those who are stronger than we are, those who have never experienced this freedom, and those who have no understanding.

~ ~ ~

We do not have to go searching for evil in some far city or upon a steep mountaintop. We do not have to look for it in someone else's life, because evil is within close range of each of us. We, as Christians, are constantly waging a battle of what will overcome in our own life:
good or evil.

The Love Chapter

But the greatest of these is charity.
1 Corinthians 13:13

I have always felt that something good lies ahead for me. It is this positive thinking that has helped me navigate through some very rough patches in life.

~ ~ ~

The clouds from the storm in my life are beginning to fade. I see God's love shining through. I think I can see the beginning of a rainbow. Yes, it is. There is going to be a rainbow in my life.

~ ~ ~

Every time I have reached out to God, my love for Him has increased.

A LOVE LETTER TO GOD

Here are some stored-up treasures from my heart that I want to share with You. I thank You every day of my life for the love I feel in my heart for You and the love I know You feel for me. I want to share my inner feelings and my entire life with You. I want to share all my littlest heartaches and all my greatest joys with You.

Thank You so much, God, for sending down Your son to die on the cross so that through His death, it is possible for You to give me Your love.

I did not realize how deep my love for You was until I had a mountain in my life. I had to reach to You first. When I asked You in a faith that never wavered to help me move this mountain, You were there. Slowly, I saw the mountain in my life move.

I have learned so much. I have learned to live one day at a time. I have learned how to walk in the Way—the Way goes before me. I have learned to follow You and listen to You because I feel You guiding me all the way through. I have learned to put Christ first in all I do and all I say. I have learned to be content in any situation I find myself—I feel that in each situation I find myself, there is a purpose. I feel that this purpose is a better understanding for others who have been in the same situation.

My life would be nothing without You. By Your being there when I needed You, You gave me a deep strength within. You came into my life and lifted me up at the right time and the right moment.

Thank You for the sweet peace I feel on the inside of me. I see so much turmoil in this world, and I want to help my friends know this peace too.

Because I love You, I want to listen intently to You. Listening closely to Your will for me helps me to know You better. I want to follow You all the days of my life. I want to submit to Your will for me in life, and I want to follow You wherever You lead me. You are Lord over my entire life.

Your love has overwhelmed me with the power to forget all the bad things in my life and has helped me look forward to a bright and shining future. I even thank You for all the bad things that have happened in my life, for through them I have become the person I am now. I realize that any confidence I feel comes from You and not from me. Before You lifted me up with Your love, I was very timid and weak. I was always afraid, especially of what others would think, but now I have no fear inside of me.

I look at the past as a learning experience. When I became more mature, You gave me Your gift of love. Thank You, God. I feel that my love for You is my commitment to You forever. You have added a new dimension to my life.

Realization of my deep love for You has brought me from death into life. Realization of my deep love for You has filled my whole being with renewed faith, overflowing joy, and a never-ending love. Realization of my deep love for You has given me a great spiritual depth, which fills my entire being.

I want to share with You some of the things I have learned.

My love for You is growing into something beautiful in my life. It is a growing kind of love. It fills me with warmth and a glow I have never felt before. When I share my inner feelings for You with others, it feels like springtime in my heart.

You are first in my life—everything else comes second. I feel closer to You than anyone in my life. My soul is nourished by just talking to You. You always listen patiently to me. When I seek advice, You give me advice through others. I have learned that this is how to obtain wisdom.

I do not fear any persecutions I may face in this life, because I know You are with me. My life ahead of me is a challenge, but I survive by living each day one day at a time, living life to the fullest in the Lord, being the best person I know to be, always being eager to learn, wanting to please You, and knowing You are always near.

Anything I think You would like for me to be, I try my best to be. I want to show others that I do care. I want to open myself to others so they can see Jesus living in me. I want to take time to listen to others. I want to reach out to others and show them love. I want to give my whole life to others. I do not have any thought of receiving anything for myself in return.

I feel that You like me the way I am. I do not have to conform to a set of rigid rules that are hard to follow, which tend only to hold back my personality and keep me from growing into the Christian You want me to be. For the first time in my life, Your love for me has helped me understand that You hate heart sins like jealousy, envy, pride, strife, bitterness, hate, stubbornness, rebellion, and self-righteousness. These are the sins that were making me die spiritually before You lifted me up.

You want me to be humble in my heart. You want me to be loving and kind. You like the real me. You accept me as I am because You know I do try to please You, and I am sincere, even though I do make mistakes along the way.

My love for You makes me feel heart-washed instead of brainwashed. I don't feel I *have* to do good to please You, but I *want* to do good from my heart so I can please You. I have no fear of not doing Your will, because I know in my heart that I am doing and living Your will instead of my own will. I feel my love for You is so deep that I can communicate to You through my thoughts, and I know Christ is living inside of me. I do meditate on Your Law of Love both day and night. This kind of love is a mystery to me.

Each morning when I wake, I find myself asking You, "God, how can I serve You today?" I feel my whole life is a ministry just serving You each day. I don't have to go to anyone but You for guidance in my life. I know that the more I give of myself, the more abundant my life becomes. Your love inspires me to be the kind of person I know You want me to be. You help me pick a lonely person out of a crowd and make him my friend. You make me feel kind in my heart. I would never want to hurt anyone intentionally. You help me love the unlovable. I want to plant seeds of kindness. I want to be a friend to everyone I meet.

You make me feel pretty in my heart. You help me pick out all the beautiful things in life. When others are down, I want to say something kind that will lift them up. I want to put others before myself. I want to praise others more and criticize others less. Sometimes, I feel You smile down at me because I do try to please You. Your love feels like rays of sunshine flowing from You into my heart.

I find myself talking to others and expressing my deep feelings for You. I can be intimate with my brothers and sisters in Christ because of the mutual Christian love we feel for each other and for You. We can express our inner selves. I feel closeness with those who love You because we share You and have so much in common. We even think alike. There is a special feeling of oneness among us. I feel togetherness, with lots of caring and sharing.

Because You love me too, I know You want all my dreams in life to come true. You have a way of lifting me up. I never feel depressed. I no longer worry, because I know You take care of the birds and, also, the flowers; I have faith that You will take care of me too. I do trust in You completely. I do not have any fear of growing old, because I know You are with me.

You are my life. I feel I am a part of You. I feel joined to You in my heart. For You, I want to look and feel my best.

I can be myself with You. I know You know me as I am. I do not have to mask any of my inner feelings, for I don't have anything to hide.

This kind of love is like a spring that flows freely, abundantly, and continues forever and ever. My life felt empty and useless before You filled it with love. Now my life feels full to the top—I feel complete.

This life on earth seems short compared to the life after death I want to spend with You. I feel that You are leading me in steps that go upward to heaven. I want to go wherever You lead me. I want to fit into Your plans for me. I want to praise You all the days of my life.

I do love You, God. I have chosen You. I want to share my entire life with You. You mean the whole world to me.

Thank You for giving me Your love and this new abundant life in Christ. You are my true friend.

Love is a spiritual relationship with God.

That so labouring ye ought to support the weak, and to remember the
words of the Lord Jesus, how he said, It is more blessed to give than to receive.

Acts 20:35

LOVE—TO GIVE, TO SUPPORT

Love is standing up for each other—offering our support, not just with our money, but lending a helping hand any time we see a need.

Love for others is treating *every* person as a special person, not just a select few.

Jesus said unto him, Thou shalt love the Lord thy God with
all thy heart, and

with all thy soul, and with all thy mind. This is the first and
great commandment.
And the second is like unto it, Thou shalt love thy
neighbour as thyself.
On these two commandments hang all the law and the
prophets.

Matthew 22:37–40

THE GIFT OF LIFE FROM A SEED

At some point in our life, the seed of God's love is planted in our heart the same as a flower seed is planted in the earth. The seed is nourished with lots of love, tender care, understanding, and gentleness, and it is watered with kindness—giving it growth.

The seed continues to bud and blossom with hope— hope for a better life.

Pain and suffering afflict us, and we reach out to God. We give Him our entire being, and we ask, "Thy will be done."

And then, with God's great mercy, the seed has grown into full bloom, a changed heart, a new life.

When we awaken to God's love within us, we want to reach out and follow His will for us. We acknowledge this love to others when we are baptized into Christ. We become joined to Him through our love. Now we are ready to begin our spiritual journey, leading us always upward through life. We go forward in faith, and we have hope for a better life, which keeps our faith strong. We start without any possessions, and anything we accumulate along the way becomes God's gift to us.

As we go on this spiritual journey, there are times we build spiritual altars to renew our commitment to Christ— each time drawing us closer and closer to God. We ask God to help us become the person He wants us to be. We may be at a funeral, and we pray, "God, I'm not ready to die yet. I want to teach others. I want to lead others to Christ." We may be sitting in church listening to a sermon, and we silently pray, "Oh, Lord, I want so much to serve You. I have a need to give more of myself to others."

We learn from our mistakes, and we profit by experience. We want to teach others so they will avoid our mistakes. We want to plant the seed of God's love in others, hoping it will grow inside of them. We want to nourish the seed of God's love with kindness, gentleness, and understanding.

As the love in us grows stronger and stronger for God, we are becoming the person He wants us to be. He molds us and makes us into what He wants us to be. We become His. Sometimes this is done through a lot of pain and suffering in our life. He wants us to be humble, kind, loving, caring, and sharing. He wants us to follow only Him and do His will—not our own will.

We start with faith. We add virtue, knowledge, temperance, patience, and godliness, and we begin loving others in our life. Everyone we meet, we find something special about them. We begin to realize that God loves everyone the same. All the experiences and mistakes we have made in life become tools for us to use in talking to others about this love. We now have understanding for others because we have been in a lot of different situations ourselves.

As the love within us grows, we become more mature, and the seed, which was once planted in our heart, begins to bloom. Every situation we find ourselves in, we begin to accept with joy because we know God has a purpose for us. We begin to look at our own experiences in life and relate them to different people in the Bible. The time we felt like a prodigal son—we came home and wanted a fresh start. The times in our life we felt like Apostle Paul—things we sincerely believed, we realized were wrong. All those times in our life, we felt like we were wandering in the wilderness, and finally, we learned to listen to God and follow Him. Biblical stories become real in our life.

All our life, all we wanted was to be loved. When God's love grows within us and reaches full bloom, we want to reach out to others and show them love. When we truly love others, we will be loved in return.

~ ~ ~

Your love, shining through the Scriptures, lights the way. It helps me comprehend more fully Your message to me.

~ ~ ~

Dad,

I was young when I left home. There were many things I did not know—I had to learn them on my own.

I have been in big-city congregations, and I have been in small congregations. I have learned so much to make me more appreciative of you and God.

It is like a breath of fresh air to be here in my home congregation. I am a free person in Christ. I can be myself. I am free to grow spiritually.

We have something here few congregations have. We have closeness between the brethren. We have a mutual Christian love for each other.

Draw nigh to God, and he will draw nigh to you. Cleanse your hands,
ye sinners; and purify your hearts.

James 4:8

PURE UNADULTERATED LOVE

Our love for God is a lifetime growing process. We grow into a mature love for God. It's an identifying process. The more mature we are in our love for God, the more we subconsciously begin to take on characteristics in our personality that we think God would like us to have. We love God—we want to be more like Him. To be more like Him, we strive to live a life without sin—a life where peace, joy, and love reign in our heart. We strive to put away our old sinful nature. We strive to make our heart pure without sin. God is love. To be more like Him, we try to pattern our life after the kind of love found in 1 Corinthians 13:4–8:

Charity suffereth long, and is kind; charity envieth not; charity vaunteth not
itself, is not puffed up, Doth not behave itself unseemly, seeketh not her own,
is not easily provoked, thinketh no evil; Rejoiceth not in iniquity, but rejoiceth
in the truth; Beareth all things, believeth all things, hopeth all things, endureth
all things. Charity never faileth.

This kind of love is a total giving of ourselves—our life. We want our life to reflect our inner self—being kind, loving, forgiving, standing up for what we think is right, and helping those in need. This kind of love lifts each other up, exalts one another, edifies. Without this kind of love, there is no hope for spiritual growth. This kind of love stands up for our brothers and sisters in Christ when they make an error and sincerely ask for forgiveness. With this kind of love, we can open up our inner selves to each other and express ourselves to help each other grow spiritually. This kind of love is free from prejudice. We are not walled in by tradition. We can open up to each other no matter who we are or where we have been in life. Rich or poor, race or creed does not matter. We become people helping people.

To grow spiritually in our love for God, we have to be willing to communicate our spiritual needs, and we have to be willing to listen—listen to God.

Our love for God can become blocked by sin, and we cannot grow spiritually. Satan puts roadblocks of sin in our spiritual path—roadblocks of selfishness (we cannot see beyond ourselves). We have the idea that the whole world revolves around us. Pride is another roadblock (the part of us that cannot face being wrong).

We are the bride of Christ. We commit adultery in our heart against God when we allow Satan to fill our heart with bitterness, guilt, selfishness, hate, pride, self-pity, and resentment. If these sins take root in our heart, then the love of God cannot flow freely from our heart outward in our life. When the love in our heart is not pure—it becomes adulterated with sin.

We love God from our heart. It is a desire. It is the individual's choice.

We, as Christians, are not out to change the world but to show the world love, and when we feel God really loves us in our heart, we will want to change our life and become like Him. The world will then change because we love one another.

~ ~ ~

Love is the key that opens the door to all hearts. Pride is the part of us that cannot face being wrong.

~ ~ ~

It is through my challenges and temptations in life that I

have been humbled.

HUMILITY

We, as Christians, do not want to admit
  failure
because a Christian is not supposed to fail.
  He is expected to succeed in life.
It is through our failures that we become
  humbled,
and only when we become humbled can we
  ever rid ourselves of pride.

Pride is an enemy of God. Pride stands in
  our path, between us and eternity.
Humbleness is living in a state of mind
  without pride.
And, in James 4:6 the Bible says,
*"God resisteth the proud, but giveth grace
  unto the humble."*

I therefore, the prisoner of the Lord.

Ephesians 4:1

A PRISONER OF OUR OWN THINKING

Lord, help us dissolve those barriers—those walls we
create in our own mind against others. Help us rid the
attitude of we are right and everyone else is wrong.

Help us to not build walls against each other but to build
strong relationships with others. Help us teach others to
become prisoners of only Jesus Christ—prisoners of His
eternal love.

Be of the same mind one toward another.

Romans 12:16

I am writing about myself. These were my thoughts and my feelings when I was a child:

HANDICAPPED STATE OF MIND

A child with a communication block lives within herself. She lives in a dreamlike existence—afraid to face her real self, afraid of being ridiculed and laughed at. She hides all her true feelings—good and bad—deep inside. She is a good child. She does everything she is told to the best of her ability. She tries to be perfect. Anything less than perfect is a failure to her. She is not honest with others. She shows a good front all the time. She is afraid of being rejected, because if she shows her true self, she reveals her weaknesses.

She cannot open up and communicate with others. She does not know how. If you have always been handicapped, you don't know there is any other way to be.

Since this child cannot express her own feelings, she goes into a behavioral pattern of letting those around her think for her. Her true feelings are hidden deep inside. She puts on a pretend front as to how she is supposed to feel. She acts the way she is taught to act. It does not come from within. She seeks praise in being a pleaser. She is weak—she does not know how to say no, and when she does, it is not very tactful. This child cannot stand up for herself. It is impossible. She cannot communicate. She does not relate her inside feelings with what she appears to be on the outside. They are two separate parts. Because of this, this child becomes so humiliated at times. She dies on the

inside.
The only way for this child to open up to others is to be shown love. She must be taught how to give it and how to receive it.

THERE'S A LITTLE OF THIS CHILD IN EACH OF US

We, as Christians, sometimes become blocked in a spiritual frame of mind. We are afraid to open up—afraid we'll be ridiculed and laughed at—so we withdraw into ourselves. We let bitterness and resentment creep into our life. We never learn to open up and express ourselves. We want to please man, so we do good works sometimes, but those works don't come directly from our heart, which causes bitterness and resentment. We feel we are being taken advantage of and used. We are afraid to say no for fear that our Christian image will be less than perfect. We feel we must walk exactly by the rules. We expect everyone else to be that way too. We become criticizers. We seek praise from man by becoming pleasers.

Slowly our heart becomes diseased—the bitterness slowly eating it away, like a cancer of the soul. We find ourselves bitter, resentful, and critical, and our spiritual growth comes to a standstill. We are spiritually blocked by sin. We slowly drift away, and we don't even realize it. The only way back to God is to be shown love—our lifeline to God, our lifeline to life. We must be shown love—how to give it and how to receive it. If we feel God really loves us, we will begin opening ourselves up to Him, and the cleansing of our sin-sick heart can begin.

~ ~ ~

When I was young, I never liked myself. I always wanted to be like my sister. God taught me to love myself for the person that I am.

SELF-ESTEEM

I am too somebody.
God made me. He made this body—this
shell that I live in.
I am not dumb. I am not stupid. I am
important. I am important to God.
He made me to be somebody.

For as he thinketh in his heart, so is he.

Proverbs 23:7

To love others, we must first love ourselves.

LOVE OF SELF IS . . .

Learning to be content with the person we are and not always wishing we were someone else.

We take a second look at ourselves, with the resources we have at hand, and we take steps to improve the foundation already laid down so we can become what we see and like in others.

~ ~ ~

We are showing love of self when we stand up for ourselves.

~ ~ ~

Authentic love is accepting me even though I am different.

~ ~ ~

Love is the desire to become our best self.

MY PRAYER IS . . .

That we might live our life so that when our Lord and Savior does come to take His loved ones (His chosen ones) home with Him, and He asks us what we did to inherit a home with Him, we can look Him straight in the eye and reply, "Lord, I truly loved You, and I did my very best."

Listening from the Heart

After my divorce, I searched to find myself and, also, to find answers to this question, "Why am I in this circumstance?" God taught me how to listen so I could receive the answers I was seeking.

EFFECTIVE LISTENING

Listening is one of the hardest lessons in life to learn. Because of human nature, we want only to listen to ourselves.

When we look up to others, we listen attentively to them. We begin to know them better by listening to what they have to say. When we begin to listen to others, we pick up a tremendous amount of information about each other. Listening to each other allows us to get inside and understand one another's feelings.

In the same manner, when we start listening to God, we become aware of what is right and wrong. We begin to have an understanding of the true nature of God.

SPIRITUAL ADVICE

Advice given to us does not do us any good if we will not listen.

For God's Word to be of any use to us in our daily life, we have to be willing to listen to the advice He gives us through the Scriptures.

~ ~ ~

We become more like our master when we lend a sympathizing ear (listening without criticism) to those who hurt, those who need emotional support, and those who need building up.

~ ~ ~

Many times, while I was going through my divorce, and afterward, I have felt the Spirit working in my life, always teaching me the difference between right and wrong.

LISTENING FOR HIS VOICE

We can hear God's voice in various ways. His voice comes to us at the beginning of an awareness of His daily presence in our life.

His voice may come as a thought, through His Word, or through our friends or our children.

His voice is there. It is soft and gentle—He speaks to us in subtle tones, it is like a cool summer breeze. He is not there, but He is there. We cannot see Him, yet we can hear

Him. We must listen.

*Let the words of my mouth, and the meditation of my heart,
be acceptable in thy sight, O LORD.*
Psalm 19:14

Each day of our life, we need a quiet time to ourselves—a moment to meditate—to commune with God. It is through these moments of deep meditation that God gives us renewed strength, His love, His understanding, and His wisdom.

Willing Working Hands

Lord, please help me surmount the tasks
You set before me without
murmuring and without grumbling.
Help me willingly accept the responsibilities
You set before me.
Help me accept defeat with dignity.
Help me always have willing working hands
for You.

DO WE REALLY LOVE GOD?

We become an unhappy slave to that which
we fear.
We become willing workers to that which
we love.

GOOD CAN OVERCOME BAD:

If we are willing to forgive.
If we are willing to forget.
If we are willing to pick out all the good
things in life instead of the bad.
If we are willing to not harbor ill feelings
toward others.

If every time someone does us a wrong, and
we, in turn, do something nice for
them.
If we are willing to squelch gossip without
passing it on.
If we are willing to show kindness instead of
hostility.
If we are willing to listen.

If we are willing to believe in ourselves,
God, and others,
good can overcome the bad in our life.

The kingdom of God is within you.
                    Luke 17:21

THE REAL YOU, THE REAL ME

Are we trying to be someone we really are
not?
Are we trying to appear to be a person on
the outside that we do not feel deep
from within?
Do we criticize others when we disagree
with them,

or do we love them enough to pray for
  them?

Do we do good works to please our minister
    or our elders, and maybe we might
    get a pat on the back,
  or do we do good works from our heart to
    please God?
Do we try to save souls merely because it
    makes us look good,
  or are we trying to save souls because we
    honestly love others?

Has our worship service become a ritual
    without any real meaning,
  or are we growing spiritually each time we
    meet with our brethren?
Are we going to church to please Mom and
    Dad so we will not humiliate them,
  or are we going to church because we truly
    are interested?

God knows.
He knows the answers to all these questions,
for the answers lie within us—
deep within our heart.

~ ~ ~

If we have never given our heart to Jesus and asked Him
to be Lord over our entire life, it will show in our daily life.
We will have a false security. Our relationship will be very
shallow. We will pretend to be someone we are not.

A Gentle and Sweet Nature

Whose adorning let it not be that outward adorning . . .
But let it be the hidden man of the heart . . . even the
ornament of a meek and quiet
spirit, which is in the sight of God of great price.

1 Peter 3:3–4

SHE LEFT A MEMORY

She died this morning. I did not know her. There were tears. They said she was the best person. She was kind and always helping others. She never spoke negatively about others. She would be greatly missed in this community.

I asked, "Was she a Christian?"

They replied, "Oh, yes."

~ ~ ~

I work for a bank in a nearby town. All my coworkers are saddened by the passing of someone they knew. I begin to think about the good influence this woman had on others. I begin to ponder and ask myself this question, "Who is the person that I admire, and who is the person that I would like to strive to become?"

Who can find a virtuous woman? for her price is far above
rubies.
The heart of her husband doth safely trust in her, so that he
shall have no need of spoil.
She will do him good and not evil all the days of her life.
She seeketh wool, and flax, and worketh willingly with her
hands.
She is like the merchants' ships; she bringeth her food from
afar.
She riseth also while it is yet night, and giveth meat to her
household, and a portion to her maidens.
She considereth a field, and buyeth it: with the fruit of her
hands she planteth a vineyard.
She girdeth her loins with strength, and strengtheneth her
arms.
She perceiveth that her merchandise is good: her candle
goeth not out by night.
She layeth her hands to the spindle, and her hands hold the
distaff.
She stretcheth out her hand to the poor; yea, she reacheth
forth her hands to the needy.
She is not afraid of the snow for her household: for all her
household are clothed with scarlet.
She maketh herself coverings of tapestry; her clothing is
silk and purple.
Her husband is known in the gates, when he sitteth among
the elders of the land.
She maketh fine linen, and selleth it; and delivereth girdles
unto the merchant.
Strength and honour are her clothing; and she shall rejoice
in time to come.
She openeth her mouth with wisdom; and in her tongue is

the law of kindness.
She looketh well to the ways of her household, and eateth
not the bread of idleness.
Her children arise up, and call her blessed; her husband
also, and he praiseth her.
Many daughters have done virtuously, but thou excellest
them all.
Favour is deceitful, and beauty is vain: but a woman that
feareth the LORD, *she shall be praised.*

Proverbs 31:10–30

SHE IS A LADY

This lady I truly admire—I look up to her. To me, she is a woman who loves God. She is a helpmeet to her husband. She loves him, and he loves her. They respect each other. She is a hard worker. She has confidence in herself. She loves her children, and her children look up to her. Christ is the center of her life. She is a person who gives of herself—her time and talents—to help others who are in need. She has the initiative to pursue her own talents. She is a kind and gracious woman. She is an intelligent person. Her beauty comes from within and shines outward for all to see.

This woman truly is a lady. I would like to pattern my life after her, and I would like to become just like her.

OUR LIFE ON EARTH IS WHAT WE MAKE IT

We can be so stingy and tight that when life is over, we have gained nothing.

We can be so frivolous and carefree that when life is over, we have wasted our entire life away.

We can live in loneliness and despair, never looking

beyond our own self and our own problems, or we can live each day for the Lord. Whatever circumstance we find ourselves in, we can accept it with gladness in our heart. And when this life is over, we will, of all men, be most richly blessed.

~ ~ ~

What good is the life we have lived, if when we are gone, we are not missed?

I pray, Lord, that I may live my life so that when I am gone—when I depart from this life—I will be missed.

~ ~ ~

We make an impression on others in our life day by day. Our life is a window reflecting to others what we are on the inside. The way we treat others is what we are in our heart.

~ ~ ~

We are separated from the world because we are Christians. Our heart is to be loving and kind.

KINDNESS

I see it in a smile.
I see it on an innocent child's face.
I see it in the eyes of an aging, gray-haired gentleman.
I see it between a boy and a girl who are very much in love.

I see it in a Christian's heart.

I see it, and I feel it
because he is different.
He is a different kind of person.

~ ~ ~

Lord, forgive me—I have not been very loving and kind in my past.

Expressions of Joy

If you have never been able to express yourself in your entire life, and suddenly you can express yourself and your feelings, you know that the joy is unspeakable and full of glory.

JOY

Oh, the joy I feel inside just being able to
    express
how I feel about myself,
how I feel about God,
and how I feel about life.

Love is to find joy
in the little things in life.
There is joy
in just living a quiet and simple life.

My thoughts turn back to the time I gave birth to my children, and I can still feel the joy I felt as a new mother.

A MOTHER'S JOY

A baby so fragile and small—
created in my own image.
God, You have made my love complete
by giving me this tiny, fragile, helpless
    human being.

Even if I did not believe in You,
I would come to believe in You.
This tiny creation is my link to Your
    existence.
How could this little miracle of life, so
beautiful, so perfect, be made by any other
than You?

Strong Family Ties

That the world may know that I love the Father.

John 14:31

YOU ARE THE BEST

Dad,

You are the best father in the whole world. I have always looked up to you. I have always felt a deep respect for you. My regard for you is felt with awe, a respectful fear, a kind of reverence in submitting to your authority. It is because I admire you and I look up to you.

I do love you, and I know you love me too. You want only what is best for me. This is why you have given me advice: so I can steer my life in the right direction to keep me from becoming a very bitter and hard-hearted person.

I feel the same kind of reverence and fear for my Father in Heaven. I look up to Him with great wonder and awe. I hold Him in high esteem. I respect His authority over me. I know He means what He says, and I know we will have a

Judgment Day. I do love God, and I fear Him. I know I want to be ready when He comes again.

His advice given to me from the Scriptures is to steer me in the right direction—to keep my heart pure.

~ ~ ~

Criticism tears down—affirmation builds up.

~ ~ ~

We can lose our individual Christian identity in church groups and organizations if we must conform to their way of thinking. We feel we must conform not because we want to or because we understand their way of thinking, but we feel we must conform to be included in a group or a party. If we conform, we are not free to be the Christian we think in our heart God wants us to be, and we cannot grow spiritually because we are not allowed to express our inner feelings for God.

UNITY IN DIVERSITY

My dear sister,

We are blood sisters in the flesh, and we are bond sisters in the Spirit. We each have the freedom to be ourselves. I do not have to conform to your personality, and I do not expect you to conform to mine.

We accept each other as we are. If I wanted to be more like you, I would have to do it on my own and not because someone forced me. If I feel I must conform to the way you think and be exactly like you, I will lose my identity.

I could not be myself. I would become a very weak person. I would be a most frustrated individual. There would be no room for growth. I would spend all my time and energy trying to be like you and blocking the real me deep inside myself. If I am free to be myself and like myself, I am free to reach maturity faster.

Our earthly father, who loves us both, wants us to be strong individuals. He does not want us to be wishy-washy. He does not want us to become doormats. He expects us to stand up for ourselves. He expects us to be ourselves.

Our earthly father allows us to express our differences. He is older and more mature. He can understand that we are on different levels of learning. He remains neutral. He realizes that for us to grow spiritually, we need to open up and express ourselves. He realizes that there are times we are going to disagree. To him, the important factor is that we disagree in a spirit of love. We know that we all three love each other. We still belong to the same family. We may not see eye to eye on some issues, but we are united because we love each other.

And I do love you, Sis.

It is the same in the spiritual realm: even in our moments of diversity, the love we, as Christians, feel for each other binds us together as one—one in Christ.

Reach out and feel the gentle touch of those who understand—those who have been where you are now.

MY FRIEND

When I was hungry spiritually, just talking
with you nourished my soul.
I was imprisoned by fear and pride—I did
not know how to escape.
You taught me to believe in myself and
God, and because of my faith, the

fear and pride disappeared.
I needed shelter in the storm of my life—
you surrounded me with love.

A man that hath friends must shew himself friendly.
Proverbs 18:24

FRIENDS

Have you ever cried heartbroken tears with those
who hurt deep inside? Have you ever
shared a humorous thought with someone,
and they thought it was humorous too?
Have you ever hurt physically when someone you
have never seen before in your life was
physically injured?
Have tears ever come to your eyes when someone
opened their heart to you, and they related
to you cruel experiences that have hurt
them emotionally?
Have you ever said, "I like you"?
Have you ever made a friend by just saying, "Hi"?
If your answer is no, it is not too late to begin.

~ ~ ~

Only when we have gone through some of the same
circumstances in life as others can we begin to have an
understanding for each other.

*Be ye angry, and sin not: let not the sun go down upon your
wrath.*
Ephesians 4:26

FORGIVENESS

When with another we are at odds,
and our whole inside cries out,
"Oh, how I wish I could get even."
What is this ill feeling that has come
between us?

We used to be friends.
I feel I have been wronged,
but, secretly inside,
I realize you feel you have been wronged
too.

Are we going to let a trifle matter destroy
our relationship?
Should I run and tell the whole world of my
hurt?
It is easy to let it slide by and sweep it under
the rug as if no ill feeling ever
existed.
That way we can both bring it out from
under the rug and bathe in self-pity
anytime and think of our resentment.

Or should I be brave and take a step
forward, forget self, and face
confrontation
so that we might dissolve this dissension—
bring out into the open what has set a gulf
between our friendship,
air out our disagreements, and put an end to
our differences?

I want you to know
you are my friend,

and I do love you.
I realize life is short—life is not easy—not
only for me but also for you.

And now is the time.
I want this wrong (if indeed I have made a
wrong) to be made right
because my Lord might
call me home this very night.

Train up a child in the way he should go: and when he is
old,
he will not depart from it.

Proverbs 22:6

CHILDREN ARE TO ENJOY

God's greatest gift of love to us is that our children are
created in our own image. They are like us. They were not
sent to us to be mistreated or abused. They are a gift to us
to be brought up in the nurture and admonition of the Lord.
We are to encourage our children, guide them, strengthen
them, correct them—always letting them know we love
them.

We, as parents, are to strive for open lines of
communication between ourselves and our children. We
need to be there when they hurt, to share their joys, and to
give them our support.

They need to be allowed to open up their inner feelings,
to express themselves, and be allowed to form their
personalities. We should allow our children to mature at
their own pace and teach them to be responsible for their
own actions.

If there is a mutual deep love between ourselves and our

children, our children will listen and follow us when we lead them because they love and trust us. We, as parents, have a responsibility of leading our children in the right direction.

Our children are ours forever—to love, to admonish, to lead. We are to enjoy our children.

I LOVE MY CHILDREN

Lord, please help me teach my children to always acknowledge You, and help me trust You to direct their path. Help them to always listen to You—that You only will be their God.

Help me teach my children to be strong individuals so they can be strong in the Lord. Help my children have the courage to say no to anything that might lead them from the path You have set before them. Help them gladly say yes to Your will.

I trust You to lead my children in the right circumstances in life, to teach them responsibility, and to teach them to be the people You want them to be.

Help me teach my children so they might come to know You in their hearts.

Please help me always be a mother to my children. Help me strive to bring out their best.

~ ~ ~

My son said to me one day, "Mom, I wish I could be famous someday."

I replied, "Son, it doesn't matter if the world views you as famous or not, because you will always be famous with me."

Somehow, I cannot help but feel this is the way God

feels about us when we become His children.

~ ~ ~

It is my utmost desire that my children should learn to get along so we might live together in harmony and peace.

It is God's utmost desire that His children should learn to get along and live together in harmony and peace.

~ ~ ~

This is what I see in my children:

VICTIMS OF CIRCUMSTANCE

We are children of divorce.
We are torn between our father and our
     mother.
We love both.
We feel a part is missing in our life.

When we are with Dad, we miss Mom.
When we are with Mom, we miss Dad.
We have done no wrong, but we feel we
     have been wronged.
We are missing out on God's plan in life—
God's plan was meant for us to be part of a
     complete family.

We are to face reality and accept this
     circumstance in our life.
There is one consolation.
We are not alone—there are millions out
     there just like us.
They are special to us because we share

something in common—
we have an understanding for each other.

Christ in Me

I am crucified with Christ: nevertheless I live; yet not I, but Christ liveth in me:
and the life which I now live in the flesh I live by the faith of the Son of God,
who loved me, and gave himself for me.

Galatians 2:20

Lord, I surrender to You myself, my life, and my will in exchange for Your Life—Your will working through me.

~ ~ ~

When I was going through my divorce, there were times I had to analyze what was most important to me. Was it worldly possessions or the peace that comes by following Christ?

SWEET PEACE

Lord, I pray that through You I may become an instrument of Your peace. Help others to see in me the inner peace I feel, which is beyond all understanding.

Those whose lives are tossed to and fro, I pray they might come to You and cast all their heavy burdens before You so they can find rest—this sweet peace within.

TO KNOW PEACE

The whole inside of me is ripped open—a storm rages in me. I cannot sleep, and I cannot eat. Then, there is a quiet calm, a stillness on the inside of me, there is peace—a rest within.

He that trusteth in his riches shall fall: but the righteous shall flourish as a branch.
Proverbs 11:28

Christ is the center of our life, or material possessions are the center of our life. To know the difference is to think, In which do I put my trust?

~ ~ ~

We often judge ourselves as to how well we have done in life by the material possessions we have obtained, by the position we hold, or by the name we have attained.

God does not measure our success with money, jobs, or a name. Success to Him is giving up our life, letting Him rule our heart, and letting Him be in complete control of our life. We are then living within His kingdom. Our reward is inner joy and inner peace.

~ ~ ~

When we are not willing to follow Christ, we become a roadblock to our own spiritual growth.

~ ~ ~

One of the biggest mistakes we make in life is letting men lead us instead of Christ.

~ ~ ~

Christ was persecuted, despised, and rejected by those who did not accept Him.

~ ~ ~

We become tangled in the web we weave around ourselves when we become law-enforcement officers trying to force God's law (as we see it) on others.

But grow in grace, and in the knowledge of our Lord and Saviour Jesus Christ.

2 Peter 3:18

When I was attending my nephew's college graduation, these thoughts came to me:

THE FRESH GRADUATE

Here I am, world. I have studied hard. I have learned all there is to learn. I am ready. Take me.

We may smile at the above statement, but we can remember when we felt the same way. When we got into the work world, we realized how little we knew and how much there was to learn. We found that the knowledge we learned in school was valuable to our employer only when we applied that knowledge to our job.

THE HONOR BIBLE STUDENT

Here I am, Lord. I have studied the Scriptures. I have memorized verses. I have read the Bible. I have learned all there is to learn. I am ready. Take me.

But we are to continue to grow in *grace* and in the knowledge of our Lord and Savior.

When we seek a relationship with our husband, children, parents, or friends, knowledge of that person (facts and history) alone does not make a relationship. The love relationship begins when we get to know that person—opening up to each other and communicating our needs to each other. When we get to know each other as we are and accept each other as we are, we are free to grow in our love for each other.

Only when we open up our inner selves to God and give Him our heart can we grow in our love for God. We can then come to know the Lord in our heart. We naturally begin to apply the knowledge of biblical principles we have gained to all areas of our own life.

Be ye therefore merciful, as your Father also is merciful.
Judge not, and ye shall not be judged: condemn not, and ye
shall not be condemned:
forgive, and ye shall be forgiven.

Luke 6:36–37

Before my divorce, I would have been included with those who have a self-righteous judgment of others when it comes to divorce.

JUDGE NOT THAT YE BE NOT JUDGED

I am writing to all my kindred brothers and sisters in Christ who have gone through the trauma of divorce, knowing our marriages cannot be worked out and wondering whether we will be lost when we face God on Judgment Day. I hope it will give you an insight into God's mercy and the infinite love He extends to us in our time of need.

We all need to be careful in our judgment of others. We may well be the one with the beam in our own eye. If we turn someone away from the doors of our congregation, we may be responsible for a soul lost—maybe many souls lost, if there are children involved. We must face reality: there are circumstances in life when a couple cannot work out their differences.

Satan wants us to live in turmoil instead of unity. If he can undermine our family life, we become weaker Christians. He works with our mind. He wants us to think that God will not forgive and that we will be eternally lost. He thrives on instilling fear inside of us. He wants to destroy any hope of Eternal Salvation—without hope, we die spiritually.

The Law of Love, written on our hearts, came into being to perfect the Old Written Code of Law. Under the old system, we were automatically cut off from God when we did not strictly adhere to the letter of the law. Under the old law, there was no forgiveness or mercy. Every *i* had to be dotted and every *t* had to be crossed.

God saw that this old system needed to be perfected, so He gave His only Son out of love. He did that specifically for you and for me so that when circumstances in our life happen, we might still be heirs with Christ in inheriting Eternal Salvation. These circumstances do happen. They are unintentional and unpremeditated. When we reach out to God, He extends us His love and His forgiveness. He picks us up and sets us back on the right path so we can follow Him.

If we use God's Word as a Written Code of Law without ever letting Christ into our heart, our heart becomes hardened, just like the Pharisees', and we become critical of each other. When we open up our heart and let Christ dwell within us, we become more forgiving of each other, and we have an understanding of each other without criticism.

And he spake this parable unto certain which trusted in
themselves that they
were righteous, and despised others: Two men went up
into the temple to pray;
the one a Pharisee, and the other a publican. The Pharisee
stood and prayed
thus with himself, God, I thank thee, that I am not as other
men are, extortioners,
unjust, adulterers, or even as this publican. I fast twice in
the week, I give tithes
of all that I possess. And the publican, standing afar off,
would not lift up so
much as his eyes unto heaven, but smote upon his breast,
saying, God be
merciful to me a sinner. I tell you, this man went down to
his house justified

rather than the other: for every one that exalteth himself
shall be abased;
and he that humbleth himself shall be exalted.

Luke 18:9–14

Christ in you, the hope of glory.

Colossians 1:27

CHRIST PERSONIFIED IN US

We are the bride of Christ. We love Him—we want to become like Him.

Our Father who art in heaven:

We pray we might come to know Your love in our heart. Help us teach others with simplicity and love so we will be listened to and understood.

When we go through trials, pain, and suffering in this life, help us meet them with strength and dignity. Help us think of only the good, which will come from our endurance.

Let us look beyond ourselves and help those who need You. Help us teach others what we have learned from our past.

Help us keep our faith strong and always stand up for You.

It is my desire to reach out and give a part of myself to others.

Help us to always have willing working hands to carry out Your will in our life. Fill us with Your gentle and sweet nature so others can see You in our lives.

Help us to always be cheerful.

Help us build strong relationships with our family and friends.

And please help us come to know You in our heart so

we might begin to think as You think in each and every circumstance. Help our love for Christ grow into a deep, true, mature love so our personality will begin to take on the characteristics of Christ, we will blend as one with Him, and He will become a living presence in our lives.

HIS ABIDING PRESENCE

Lord, when I opened my eyes this morning, I saw the sunlight streaming onto my pillow, and I felt Your presence.

I went to church this morning, and as I was singing, I felt a deep communion between myself and You, Lord.

Again, I felt Your presence as I viewed with awe the beauty of some of the marvelous works only You could create—I overlooked a valley, a river winding far below, I saw the trees touching the sky on a hill far away.

I talked to a sister in Christ today—we shared our love for You—and You were there in our midst. Later, I was all by myself, but I did not feel alone.

This day is over. Now it is time to close my eyes—I know I can sleep well. I feel safe. I am at peace because You are still here—Your presence has become a part of me.

When we walk with Christ through life, we will never have to walk alone. Even when we are alone in a crowd, we are not alone—He is there beside us.

~ ~ ~

The people in my life whom I deeply love have become a part of me, and their memory and presence can be felt even years after their death or long periods of separation.

LOVE IS STRONGER THAN DEATH

You are not just a memory.
You are a living presence.
You have become a part of me.

Reflections on Life After Divorce

MY IDENTITY

I do not feel I have lived my life for naught,
because of the vast knowledge I have gained from
my past.
Memories of faces in other times and places
make up the identity of who I am now.

WORDS OF ADVICE

From this day forth
keep in front only the memories of good times.
Leave the bad moments behind.
We are to use the knowledge we have gained from
our experiences in life by teaching others,

and our life will have purpose—it will take on new meaning.

These are my thoughts about my failed marriage:

REFLECTING BACK

In thumbing through the pages of memory in my mind, I stumbled across a moment when I was young, and I saw in you a kind and good heart.

I also remember that I felt there was no need for any change in myself. I thought that since we were both Christians, our relationship would grow into something deep and lasting. I did not know any different.

Over the years, my relationship with Christ has deepened, and my heart has changed. I can see that God's way is loving, forgiving, merciful, and kind toward His children.

I like to think that up until now, my life has been filled with stepping-stones, for I feel I have gotten in touch with myself, with God, and with the world. I feel I have become a better person.

~ ~ ~

I have come to the realization that most of my problems in my failed marriage stemmed from my own immaturity.

MATURITY

When I was young, I drew a circle around myself, and I could only relate to those who came close to being just like me.

I am now older and more mature. The circle has dissolved completely—everyone I meet I can relate to because I see a part of myself in each person.

For every mistake I make in life, if I can learn a lesson, the error will not have been made in vain, and I will be able to live better tomorrow than I did today.

THE PATCHWORK QUILT

My life is likened unto a patchwork quilt: all the patches and pieces, some torn but sewed back together with loving and caring hands, have been sewed with the fine thread of His love and His patience so that when my life is over, it will be finished—completed to His liking.

A Closing Thought

MY DAUGHTER NEEDING ACCEPTANCE
AT AGE NINE

I look beyond that long mop of hair I am constantly reminding you to comb.

And, as I look, I can see beneath that rebellious nature, which is commonly found in the young and in the old.

I can see a person, an individual, with a good heart wanting only to be loved, understood, and respected on her level—not mine.

You are telling me by your actions:

Don't talk to me of what you want me to be or what you want me to do because I am not interested.

I want only to be accepted by my peers.

I will do anything in order to have friends, even if it takes wearing the same jeans or cutting my hair exactly like my friends'—it horrifies me to think that someone might label me as being different.

After concentrating on these things, I realize you are just

like the rest of us. We do not like to be told what to do. We want to do what we want.

And, as I look even closer—as I put myself on your level—I can understand that you are only trying to find yourself. You are torn between cutting loose from Mom's apron strings and springing forth on your own two feet. Sometimes you cling to me, and at other times, you reject me.

Then, it suddenly dawns on me—it is up to me to teach you.

To teach you that we are not always going to be accepted by everyone and that we cannot be what everyone else thinks we should be. We should only be ourselves, and if we are not accepted by our peers and our family, we have not lost a friend, because that person was never a friend to begin with.

At night before we go to bed, when we laugh and hug each other, I whisper into your ear, "You are my favorite daughter." I believe you know I love you and I want only what is best for you.

And, if I, as a parent, can shower you with a little more patience and understanding and look beyond the present, I can see that you are going to grow into a fine young lady. You will go through changes—your years ahead of you will not be easy, but you will experience growth physically, mentally, emotionally, and spiritually. If you do not grow in all these areas, I will know immediately that something is wrong somewhere.

By the time you are twenty, we will be able to read these same words and see the changes that have taken place in your life from now until then.

You will have taken a great step toward maturity.

~ ~ ~

At night after I turn off the lights, I lie in bed thinking. I look back over the past ten years of my life, and as I take a closer look at the spiritual side of my life, I find myself asking, "That rebellious nature I have, has it been subdued? Have I taken steps in my life to overcome the tendency to be a pleaser to be accepted? Am I constantly growing spiritually? Have I taken on a more positive attitude toward life?"

When I answer these questions all in the affirmative, I know in my heart that I am a Christian. And I begin to realize that God does love me. He wants me to be a happy individual. He wants only what is best for me in life.

~ ~ ~

Growth requires change!

Acknowledgments

Thank you, Callie Walker. I recognize your gift of insight, and I am grateful for the advice you have given me in the final stages of this book. I would also like to thank Connie Martin. You have encouraged me to move forward on my journey to publish my book.

Thank you, Sharon Kizziah-Holmes, for helping me fulfill my lifelong dream of becoming a published author.

~ ~ ~

I am grateful to everyone I have met through the years who have inspired me to want to change to become a better person.

Elaine Anderson: after attending Elaine's Bible classes, I wanted *to turn my life around and ask the Lord to help me.*

Carol Baker, my friend: I respect the *dignity and strength* she displayed through the loss of her son.

Lorraine Munger: I admire her *deep faith in God and her willingness to stand up for that faith.*

The Apostle Paul: He was a most sincere person. When he came to know the truth in his heart, he did not put his light under a bushel. He had a burning *desire to spread the truth to others,* which often meant risking his own life.

Fred Killebrew: He was a preacher. He preached with *simplicity and a love for God* that even as a child I could understand, and I listened to him attentively.

My mother, Marjorie Martin: she has always been a

willing and hard worker all her life.

Leota King, my children's grandmother, and Lucille Porter, my aunt: they are both very *loving and kind* people.

Lennie Thurman: she is a *kind and gracious* lady—her beauty comes from within and shines out into the hearts of those who know her.

Lorene Plemmons, a wife and a mother: She passed away from this life many years ago. She is still *loved and missed* by those who knew her.

Madonna Schacht, my friend: I will always remember her *enthusiasm and joy for life.*

Mary Jones, my friend: she taught me that we can *use our past as a learning experience to teach others.*

My family: they have shown me true Christianity by helping me when I needed help, and I thank them for their *continued love and support.*

My great-grandmother Valera Jane Hightree: In her older years she was blind, and during this time in her life she, for the most part, *lived independently.* I still remember the *closeness* I felt to her.

Christ: He is my Lord, my Savior, my Redeemer—He gave His life for me. I love Him because He first loved me. His love is a self-giving love. Whatever state I may be in (lonely, poor, miserable wretch that I may be), He gave Himself out of a self-giving love for me so that I may be delivered from that state of mind and that I, too, may learn to love by His example and give myself—my love—to others. Just realizing His self-giving love for me, the least I can do is turn my life around and live for Him, not for myself, and try to become my best for Him.

To those listed above, you have touched my life. You have made a deep impression on my soul. It is my prayer and my desire that I might change to become what I have seen in you.

About the Author

At the time *Undying Embers of God's Love* was written, Janet lived in a small town in central Missouri with her two children. Janet has always considered her life a journey. She feels she has learned from her own mistakes, and she has learned from others. A part of her journey has been writing her thoughts and feelings on paper and writing her first book. She feels it is a sacred honor to be a daughter of God. Janet is currently working on her second book.